TOO NiCE

SALLY NiCHOLLS

Barrington  Stoke

Published by Barrington Stoke
An imprint of HarperCollins*Publishers*
Westerhill Road, Bishopbriggs, Glasgow, G64 2QT

www.barringtonstoke.co.uk

HarperCollins*Publishers*
Macken House, 39/40 Mayor Street Upper,
Dublin 1, DO1 C9W8, Ireland

First published in 2024

ISBN 978-1-80090-326-5

10 9 8 7 6 5 4 3 2 1

A catalogue record for this book is available from the British Library

Printed and Bound in the UK using 100% Renewable Electricity
at Martins the Printers Ltd

This book contains FSC™ certified paper and other controlled
sources to ensure responsible forest management.

For more information visit: www.harpercollins.co.uk/green

CONTENTS

Chapter 1
TOO NICE!

"My stepmother's all right," said Abby. "She's just too nice. That's all. Too nice!"

"Urgh," Anna replied. She tipped her crisp packet up so all the last crumbs fell into her mouth. They were sitting in their corner of the canteen at school. "You mean she's all goody-two-shoes and perfect?"

"No ... not exactly," Abby said. She opened her lunchbox and stared at the lunch her stepmother, Jen, had made her. Cheese sandwiches with lettuce. A Fruit Corner. Grapes. Cherry tomatoes, and cucumber cut into little cubes. Posh food. It was much nicer than the packed lunches Abby used to make for herself. "It just feels *fake*."

"Yuck," said Finn. He was eating chips covered in ketchup. Abby used to eat chips covered in ketchup too. Before Jen moved in.

"I wish my stepmother was *too nice*," said Halima gloomily. "Mine is always going on at me. *Halima, tidy your room. Halima, do your homework. Halima, tell your brothers to stop killing each other, will you? I can't do everything on my own.*"

"I like your stepmother," said Abby. She did. Halima's stepmother was always bossing Halima around, but you could tell they loved each other really. "She's *real*," Abby added.

"Too real," said Halima. "I wish she would be fake nice to me sometimes. It would make a change!"

Abby's mum had died when she was little. Abby couldn't remember her at all. Her dad told her lots of stories. And she had a picture of her that she liked to look at sometimes. But that was it.

Abby had never really minded not having a mum. She liked that she and Dad made decisions together. They talked about things, like where they should go on holiday and what takeaway to order. They were a team.

They liked the same things too. They played video games together. They watched TV. Dad liked *Doctor Who* episodes from the 1960s and old *Star Trek*. Abby liked the way he got all excited when he talked about them. She liked teasing him about the bad special effects. She liked introducing him to the things she loved too. They watched all the Marvel films and TV programmes together. Dad pretended not to like them, but he did really.

Abby and Dad were friends. Their family was small, but it *worked*.

And then Jen came along.

Jen was Dad's girlfriend. They'd been together for six months now. He'd had girlfriends before. But Abby had been little then. She hadn't understood what was going on. She'd just thought he had a new friend who was a lady.

This time, Abby had been excited about meeting Jen. Abby loved her dad. She wanted him to be happy. She thought it was cool that he had a girlfriend. She helped him tidy the house. She even bought some tulips and put them in a vase on the table. They looked so nice there, red and hopeful.

Jen was a librarian. She worked at the school where Dad was a teacher. She was small and pretty, with short dark hair and dangly earrings.

Jen talked a lot.

Abby opened the door the first time Jen came over, and Jen started talking.

"Abby! How lovely!" Jen cried. "I've been so excited about meeting you. I've heard so much about you! Your dad's so proud of you! Well, you know that."

Jen stepped forward and held out her arms for a hug. Abby hadn't expected that. She wasn't sure what to do. She didn't mind being hugged. But this was the first time they'd met. Wasn't hugging a bit full on for a first meeting?

It felt rude to say so. She let Jen hug her. But she felt herself getting small and shy, which wasn't at all how she'd wanted to behave. She knew Dad was proud of her. He was *her* dad. Why was Jen acting like she knew him better than Abby did?

"Oh, I love your top!" Jen was still talking. "That blue really suits you – it matches your eyes."

"Thank you," Abby said again. It was just an old top. It wasn't anything special. There was an ink stain on the hem. She wanted to say this to Jen, but she thought it might sound rude. It made her feel funny though, as if Jen was lying to her.

"Why don't you come inside?" said Dad, moving into the house.

Jen and Abby followed. Abby was still trying to work out why Jen made her feel so uncomfortable. Dad hardly ever said things like "I love your top". Only if she was wearing something really special, like a dress for a wedding or something. Was it just because Jen was a woman? Would Abby's mum have said, "Oh, what a lovely top!" if she'd been alive?

Did Jen really mean it, or was she just trying to make Abby like her?

"Oh, I love your top" was a *nice* thing to say to someone.

So why did it make Abby feel so small?

Jen was still talking. "What a lovely house! Oh, and tulips! I love tulips!"

"They were Abby's idea," said Dad. Abby wished he hadn't said that. She waited for Jen to start telling her how much she loved tulips.

"I love tulips!" Jen said, right on cue. "They're so cheerful, aren't they? They remind me of my grandmother – she always had tulips in the garden when we went to visit. What a kind thought!"

Abby had chosen the tulips because they were the smallest bunch of flowers in the shop, and she and Dad only had little vases. She didn't say this. She changed the subject.

"This is the kitchen," Abby said. "And this is the garden."

But it was the same wherever they went. Jen *gushed*. About Abby. About the house. About Dad.

"I'm so happy to finally meet you!" Jen kept saying. She filled the whole house with her words.

And Abby felt smaller and smaller, and more and more squashed.

Chapter 2
MOVING IN

After that, Jen started spending a lot more time at their house. She would come over at the weekend. She would come home from work with Dad after school. She and Dad started doing things together. Dad joined Jen's choir. They started going on long walks at the weekend.

"You can come too, Abby!" Jen said. "We'd love to have you with us!" But Abby never knew if she could believe her.

"It's all right," Abby said, feeling awkward.

"You're getting too grown up to do things with your old dad, are you?" Dad said. He was smiling, but his words made Abby feel funny inside. She *wasn't* too grown up. She *liked* doing things with Dad. She knew teenagers weren't supposed to want to do things with their parents. But Abby had never felt like that. She *loved* her Dad.

There was something about the way Dad said it which worried her. It was as if he thought Abby *should* be too grown-up.

Did he even want her on the walk with them?

"You don't mind us going, do you?" Dad said.

"No, of course not," said Abby. "Go. Have fun!"

But she did mind. She missed Dad being *hers*.

Abby knew she was being selfish. She knew she wasn't being fair. Dad still loved her. He told her he loved her all the time. Every day. And Jen was nice. Abby knew she was nice.

"I always wanted a daughter!" she said to Abby.

I'm not your daughter, Abby thought. But she didn't say it out loud. She didn't want to be a brat. She wanted to be a nice person. She *was* a nice person.

"We should do something just the two of us!" Jen said. "A mother-daughter trip! Not that I am your mother, of course. I know you've got a mother. But you know what I mean!"

"I don't have a mother," said Abby flatly.

"No, but ... I don't want to disrespect your mother's memory," Jen said. "You know that, don't you?"

"I suppose," Abby said. Jen wasn't disrespecting her mum's memory. But she was shoving herself into the space Mum had left behind.

"So, what would you like to do?" Jen said. She looked at Abby, waiting. How was Abby supposed to know? She'd never had a mum before.

"I dunno," she said.

"You must have some ideas?" said Jen. "What do you do with your dad?"

"Go to the cinema," Abby muttered. She wished Jen would stop this. "We could go and see the new Marvel film?"

"Oh," Jen said. "I don't really like Marvel ... and I know your dad was looking forward to taking you to that."

"Oh," said Abby.

"We could go to the theatre!" said Jen. "Or are there any bands you like? I haven't been to a concert in years! Or we could have afternoon tea?"

"Um." Abby felt smaller and smaller. "Sure. OK. The theatre, maybe?" She didn't want to go to a concert with Jen. At least they wouldn't have to talk in the theatre.

Jen took her to see *Mamma Mia*. She talked all the way there about how excited she was.

"I love *Mamma Mia*!" Jen said. "Have you seen the film version? I used to love ABBA when I was your age. I knew all the songs!"

Abby didn't know what to say.

"Dad and I mostly watch science-fiction films," she said. Jen looked a bit disappointed, so Abby added, "But I like other things too!"

"My mum died when I was twelve," said Jen. "Did I tell you that? She used to take me to the theatre all the time."

"I'm sorry," said Abby.

"It was a long time ago," said Jen. "And now I have you!" She smiled at Abby.

Abby wanted to cry.

*

Abby knew she was lucky to have a stepmother who tried so hard. She should be grateful, she told herself. And she did try. Abby smiled politely when Jen and Dad said how sensible she was being. That was the problem with being sensible. You weren't allowed to complain.

Abby *wanted* to be sensible.

She just hadn't expected Jen to *move in*.

"Jen is pretty much living here already," Dad said. "She stays most weekends ... so it just makes sense for her to live here. Doesn't it?"

He gave Abby a hopeful smile. It made her heart hurt to look at him. She didn't want to let him down.

"I suppose so," Abby said.

"Are you sure?" Dad said. "You don't mind? You like Jen, don't you?"

Abby forced herself to smile.

"Of course I like her," she said weakly. "She's lovely."

Dad looked pleased.

"She is, isn't she?" he said. "I can't believe she wants to be with a boring old man like me!"

"You aren't boring!" said Abby.

Dad laughed. "But I am old?"

"Well ..." Abby didn't finish the sentence. He was a dad. All dads were old. Surely he knew this?

"Cheeky so-and-so," Dad said. He gave Abby a fond look.

"Thank you for being so good about this," he said. "I'm so lucky to have you."

"Me too," she said. She tried to ignore the part of her that wanted to be un*sensible*. The part that wanted to be childish and immature about it.

Dad was allowed to have girlfriends.

This would be OK. It would.

*

And it was OK. Jen wasn't a Wicked Stepmother.
She didn't steal Dad's money, or lock Abby in the
cellar. She carried on being, well, *nice*.

But it still felt strange having another person
living in their house. Jen wasn't a stranger. But
she wasn't *family*.

Abby was used to having lots of time on her
own. Dad often stayed behind after school to
finish his marking. He said he wanted to leave
work at work and be a dad at home. Abby got a
bit lonely sometimes, but she didn't really mind it.
It was nice having some quiet time after school.
She did her homework, messed about on the
internet and watched all the TV shows that Dad
didn't like.

But that all changed when Jen moved in. Jen
didn't have marking to do or staff meetings to go
to like Dad did. She got home at four o'clock every
day. Sometimes she was home before Abby was.

Abby hated it.

It felt as if her private time and space was
being invaded. Abby liked school, but it was
hard work. You couldn't relax. You had to be
nice to your friends and pay attention to what
teachers said. You had to make sure you didn't

say anything stupid. It was exhausting. Abby had never realised how much she *needed* time on her own. Time when she didn't have to pretend. Time when she could just *be*.

Their house wasn't very big – it only had two bedrooms. Even when Abby was in her room, she could still hear Jen downstairs moving around, singing to herself. And Jen was so *friendly*. So talkative. Abby wasn't used to that. If Abby went downstairs to get a drink or something, Jen would stop whatever she was doing and want to chat.

"Abby! Hello! Do you want a cup of tea? We could have some biscuits. Or a teacake?"

Jen would look hopefully at Abby. Abby never knew what to say. She just wanted to make a glass of squash and go back to her room. But she couldn't work out how to say that without being rude. So, she'd have to sit there, drinking tea, feeling ... squashed.

Once, she said something – she couldn't help it. Jen was babbling away as normal.

"How's your homework going?" she said. "You're doing so well. Your dad and I are so proud of you!"

Why did Jen say things like that? *Your dad and I.* Jen and Dad weren't a family! She was just Dad's girlfriend! She didn't get to say things like *your dad and I.*

"Why do you think I'm doing well?" Abby said. She didn't mean it to sound so blunt. It just came out like that.

"Oh!" Jen said. She didn't seem upset. She was *always* cheerful. "Well, your dad said you were ever so clever. And I can see that you get on with your homework every day ..."

Abby *did* do her homework every day. But that didn't mean she was clever! It sounded fake when Jen said it.

"How do you know what I'm doing?" Abby said. "I could be up to anything. Computer hacking! Online trolling! Internet piracy!"

Jen laughed, but it sounded anxious.

"Oh, well, yes, I suppose you could be," she said. "Now! Would you like Hobnobs or chocolate digestives with your tea?"

If someone was nice to you, you were supposed to be nice to them back. Abby knew that. But if Abby was nice back, then that would just encourage Jen. There would be even more niceness! And Abby didn't want that. She wanted less nice! But the only way to get that was by being nasty.

Abby didn't want to be nasty. She wasn't a nasty person! She was friendly and kind to everyone else. Why couldn't she be nice to Jen?

Just back off, Abby wanted to say. *I don't want a mother. Can't you just be a … a person?*

Chapter 3
NICE THINGS

And lots of things *were* better with Jen in the house.

Jen was good at tidying up and hoovering. She always remembered to buy milk and bread. There was fancy fruit in the fruit bowl. Kiwis and grapes and even a pineapple once. Jen cooked a lot more than Dad did too. Mostly Dad made soup or sandwiches or bacon butties for tea.

But Jen cooked proper dinners. Vegetarian chilli. Stir fries. Home-made pizza. When Abby came home from school, the whole kitchen smelled of good things cooking.

The house was nicer too. Dad always used to leave the dirty dishes on the side until they ran out of clean forks. Now, they did the washing-up every night. Jen changed the sheets on Abby's bed every week. She hoovered the house every couple of days. And she made Dad and Abby help too.

"Abby, love, can you tidy up all this mess in the living room, please?" she'd say. And Abby would.

"I'll wash; you dry," she would say to Dad. And Dad would too.

Jen was trying to make their house a proper home. Abby could see how much work it was, and she knew it was a good thing. She should be grateful, she knew.

Jen was also keen on *doing* things. She said things like, "Let's go on a picnic!" Or "Look, there's a free festival in town, shall we go?" Dad didn't really have hobbies, but Jen did. Jen liked books, and walking, and theatre, and films. She was in a choir. She collected this old-fashioned series of books called *The Chalet School*. She had a lot of friends. She had a real, full, interesting life. Dad didn't have a life like that. Abby had never really noticed or minded before. But friends and hobbies and cooked dinners were a good thing. Maybe she and Dad had been missing out by not doing those things.

Abby liked that Dad was happy. But the nice things felt hard sometimes. For example, Jen had brought round all this stuff from her old flat. She'd replaced their sofa with her own. She'd taken down some of the pictures and put up new ones. She'd thrown Dad's old duvet cover away. She'd put all the old ornaments away too.

Abby knew she shouldn't complain about this. This was Jen's house now. She was allowed to have her own pictures on the walls and books in the bookcases. Abby knew that. She knew it.

But … but … but …

But this was the house Mum and Dad had lived in before Abby was born. Her mum's stuff was all over the house. Her books on the bookcases. The pictures she had chosen on the walls. The ornaments Jen put away had belonged to Mum. It wasn't that Abby liked them much. They were twee and silly. But they were *Mum's*.

Abby didn't know much about Mum. Dad talked about her of course. And so did Gran and Grandpa. But talking wasn't the same as knowing.

It was as if Abby had found out about Mum from her things. Mum liked the Beatles, and so did Abby. She liked Diana Wynne Jones, and Abby did too. She'd liked finding that out for herself. She had some of Mum's jewellery, which she wore sometimes. Dad had kept all Mum's clothes. Abby had even worn some of her T-shirts. She thought she might wear more of Mum's clothes when she got older.

But they were all gone now. Jen's clothes were in the wardrobe, and Mum's clothes were in the attic.

Abby felt ridiculous that she minded so much. She couldn't even remember Mum! And it wasn't as if Jen had thrown anything away. She'd been so careful about that. Abby could have got Mum's things down from the attic if she'd asked. But she felt weird making a fuss about it.

Of course Jen should put her own clothes in her own wardrobe. Of course she should put her own pictures on the wall. Abby had never cared what pictures were on the wall before. They were all boring grown-up pictures! Jen hadn't done anything wrong. She really, really hadn't.

So why did it feel as if Jen was pushing Abby out?

It felt like Jen was redrawing the map of her family. First it had been Mum and Dad and Abby. Then Abby and Dad. Now it was Jen and Dad, with Abby off to one side somewhere.

Abby knew she was being unfair. But that was what it felt like sometimes.

Chapter 4
NERVOUS

Abby had tried to talk to Dad about Jen.

"She's just nervous," said Dad.

"Nervous!" said Abby. Jen wasn't nervous. Jen was always talking and talking and talking. How could she be nervous?

"Jen wants you to like her," said Dad. "She wants you to know that she likes you."

"I do know that," said Abby. "She doesn't need to tell me how great I am. She said it seven times last night! I counted."

"She's being nice," said Dad. He sounded a bit annoyed, as if he was on Jen's side. Abby felt guilty.

"I do like her," Abby said. "You know I do. I just ... it's too much. It feels fake."

"I understand," said Dad. "It takes a bit of getting used to, doesn't it? But Jen isn't pretending. She's like this with everyone."

"But I already know she likes me," said Abby. "She doesn't have to keep telling me."

"She's worried," said Dad. "She's a bit insecure."

"Insecure!"

It seemed such an odd thing to say about a grown-up. Kids were insecure. Not grown-ups. And why would a grown-up be insecure about whether a kid liked them? Why would a grown-up even care?

"Yes, insecure," said Dad. "Adults are human beings too. Jen wants us to be a family."

"But we're not a family," Abby said. As she said it, this seemed like the most important point. "Jen is pretending we are, but we aren't. Family is people you're related to. You, me, Gran and Grandpa – we're family."

"I'm not related to Gran and Grandpa," Dad pointed out. "And I wasn't related to your mum. Family can be people you choose too."

"You know what I mean," Abby said.

"And you know what I mean," said Dad.

"OK," Abby said. "I take your point. But you can't just decide to be someone's family. You have to earn it."

Dad looked like he was trying very hard not to say something. Abby supposed he was thinking about all the dinners Jen cooked and school uniforms she washed. But she'd never asked Jen to do any of it.

Dad took a deep breath. "I agree," he said, in an odd voice, as if he was trying to be polite. "But she can't earn it if you won't let her, can she?"

*

Abby did try. She smiled at Jen. She was polite. But she kept feeling herself pulling back.

Their relationship felt like a set of scales. Or a tug of war. It felt like Jen wanted to be best friends with Abby straight away. Abby wanted her to back off a bit. It wasn't that she wanted them to be enemies. Just ... people who liked each other and lived in the same house and gave each other space.

That was all she wanted, really. Some space.

And some time.

Chapter 5
A HOLIDAY

Before Jen moved in, Abby saw a lot of her gran and grandpa. They lived about ten minutes' drive away and had always been very involved in her life. When she was little, they looked after her while Dad was at work. They came to all her school plays and birthday parties. Abby had always thought of them as extra parents.

Real extra parents.

Gran and Grandpa were trying to be nice about Jen. But Abby could tell they were a bit upset about her. Abby could see why. Mum was their daughter. It must have been weird for them to see Dad with someone else. They didn't come round so much after Jen moved in. Abby was sad about that. She loved her grandparents.

When Gran and Grandpa did come round, things were different. Jen insisted on cooking proper meals for them. They had wine. It felt more ... formal. More like guests and less like family.

Why did Jen get to make those choices? Gran and Grandpa weren't *her* family. They were Abby's.

Gran and Grandpa came round to dinner that Sunday.

"Jen's a nice girl, but she does talk a lot, doesn't she?" Grandpa whispered to Abby as they laid the dining table. Abby smiled at him, grateful he'd noticed.

"She does a bit," Abby whispered back. It was nice to have someone on her side for once.

"Oh, that's wonderful!" said Jen, coming into the kitchen. "Thank you so much for laying the table! What an amazing job you've both done!"

"It's nothing really," Abby muttered.

Grandpa looked at Jen. "There's no need to talk to me like that," he said. "I'm not five years old, you know! I know how to lay a table!"

Jen immediately started apologising. "Oh, I'm so sorry!" she said. "I didn't mean it like that! I'm just so pleased! It's a real help!"

"I had four kids of my own," Grandpa said. "There's no need to patronise me."

Jen started talking even faster.

"Oh, I wasn't patronising you! Honestly! I know you can lay a table! It's just so nice to have guests who help!"

"Hmph," Grandpa said. He still looked cross. Abby wasn't sure what to think. She didn't want Jen to be upset. But it was nice to know that Grandpa felt the same as her. It *was* patronising to be told over and over how wonderful it was to lay a table.

Jen was still gabbling on.

"Really, I think you're wonderful. You both are! That's not what I meant at all!"

"All right," said Grandpa. "Fine." But he didn't sound fine.

After that, dinner was a bit awkward.

"We need to talk about holidays," said Gran. Abby and Dad always went on holiday with Gran and Grandpa. "We thought maybe that resort in Spain again? What do you think?"

"Yes!" said Abby. She liked Spain. They'd stayed in a cool hotel with a pool and a beach nearby.

Dad and Jen looked at each other.

"Well ..." said Dad. "Jen and I were thinking we might do something else this year. It's so kind of you to include us in your holidays, but we thought you might like the chance to do something on your own."

Abby stared at Dad.

"But we always go on holiday with Gran and Grandpa!" she said.

"I know," said Dad. "But things are different now."

Gran and Grandpa looked just as shocked as Abby felt.

"Well," said Gran. "If that's how you feel ... We won't stand in your way."

"It isn't like that," said Jen, but Abby knew it totally was like that. "We just thought you might want the chance to get away just the two of you."

"I like going on holiday with Gran and Grandpa," said Abby. She was horrified. Jen couldn't take her grandparents away from her ... could she?

"We like going on holiday with you, sweetheart," Gran said.

Dad's smile was fading.

"Well, of course, if you feel like that ..." he said.

Jen interrupted, "If Abby wants to go on holiday with you, I'm sure she could go on her own," she said.

Abby felt like she'd been slapped in the face. Would this be instead of a holiday with Jen and Dad? Jen hadn't said that ... but it felt like she was splitting them apart again. Dad and Jen on one side. Abby on the other.

At least this time she wasn't alone – she was with Gran and Grandpa.

"Yes!" Abby said. "Can I?"

Dad looked a bit shocked.

"I suppose so," he said. "If Gran and Grandpa don't mind."

"We'd love you to come on holiday with us," said Gran firmly.

Abby wanted to stick her tongue out at Jen. *So there, Jen. Nobody likes you.*

"Well! Isn't that lovely?" said Jen. She was still trying to pretend everything was OK. But nobody looked fooled.

*

When Gran and Grandpa had gone, Jen sat down on the sofa and said, "Oof!"

Dad took her hand.

"That went about as well as could be expected," he said.

"I didn't upset them, did I?" said Jen.

Yes, Abby thought.

"They'll get over it," said Dad.

Abby wasn't so sure. Now she felt like she had a real excuse to be angry with Jen. It wasn't fair to push Grandpa and Gran out of their holidays.

Abby scowled at Dad, who said, "Do you have something you want to say, Abby?"

"No," said Abby sulkily.

"Oh, Abby, I'm sorry," said Jen at once. "You don't mind, do you? I just don't think your grandparents would really want to go on holiday with me. They don't really know me. And it would be nice to have a holiday just the three of us, wouldn't it?"

Jen and Dad both looked at Abby. So she wasn't banned from the family holiday. She was so relieved – she'd thought they didn't want her.

"Sure," Abby said. "Yeah. Fine. OK."

But it wasn't OK. And Dad should have known that.

Chapter 6
A PRIZE

The next day, something else happened.

Dad and Jen came home from school together. This was unusual.

"Abby!" Dad called as they came through the door. "We've got fish and chips!"

Abby came downstairs. She and Dad used to get fish and chips a lot. They didn't have it so much now Jen was here. Jen thought chips were unhealthy.

"We're celebrating," said Dad. He kissed Abby. "Jen won an award!"

"What sort of award?" said Abby. She was still angry about Gran and Grandpa not coming on holiday with them. She didn't feel like she wanted to congratulate Jen.

"Best school librarian," said Jen. She looked flushed and happy. "It's a local thing – just for our area. They're awards for people who work in schools. One of the sixth formers nominated me – I didn't even know about it!"

"Very well deserved," said Dad. He put his arm around her. They both looked at Abby, waiting for her to say something.

"Wow," said Abby. "I mean – congratulations."

"There's a ceremony," Jen said. "Isn't that funny? It's at school and they're going to present the awards and things – the mayor's going to be there! Family are invited. You will come, won't you, Abby?"

No, thought Abby. She didn't want to. She didn't want to have to always pretend.

"When is it?" Abby said. She went over to the cupboard and took out some plates so she wouldn't have to look at Jen any more.

"A week on Friday," said Jen. "In the school hall! Please come, Abby. I'll be so nervous. It'll make me feel so much better knowing you and your dad are there."

But why? thought Abby crossly. It still didn't make sense to her. *I'm not your daughter!* she wanted to shout. *Why does it matter if I'm there or not?*

"I can't," Abby said, without thinking about it.

There was a sudden, shocked silence behind her. Abby never said *I can't.*

"Why?" said Dad.

Why couldn't she?

"Halima's having a party," Abby said. She took the plates over to the table and began to lay them out.

"I thought Halima's birthday was in June?" said Dad.

"It's not her birthday party," said Abby. "It's because ..." Why would Halima have a party? "Just because. I don't know."

"Because her parents are away from home?" said Jen. It sounded like an accusation. Abby was so surprised by the question, she turned around. Jen was always enthusiastic and happy. It wasn't like her to be suspicious.

"No!" Abby said. "They're going to be there. They always are. Halima's stepmum is really strict. Isn't she, Dad?"

"That's true," said Dad. Was he suspicious too? She couldn't tell.

"I think it's because Halima didn't have a birthday party," Abby said, before Jen could start suggesting they ring Halima's parents. "So, this is a late one. I can go, can't I?"

There was a small pause. Dad looked like he wanted to argue. Then Jen said brightly, "Of course you can go." She gave Abby a small smile. "It's a shame you can't come to the ceremony, but that's just the way it is, isn't it?"

Something about her voice made Abby feel awful.

But it was too late now.

"I am sorry," she said. "I would come if I could."

"Of course you would, sweetheart," said Jen. She kissed Abby. "I know that."

Dad gave Abby an odd look. Abby put the glasses on the table, trying not to look at Jen or Dad. For the first time, she felt like the villain.

And she didn't like it at all.

*

After that, something changed. Abby wondered if she was the only one who felt it.

She stopped trying to be polite and nice all the time. And that was OK, actually. Jen had told Gran and Grandpa they couldn't come on holiday! She had taken all of her mum's clothes out of the wardrobe! Jen wasn't a nice person. It was OK for Abby not to like her. It was *normal*!

But even as she thought it, she knew it wasn't true. Jen was trying so hard. She was really kind and helpful. Abby knew it was a bit odd for Dad to keep Mum's clothes in a wardrobe years after she had died. She even understood why Jen wouldn't want to go on holiday with Gran and Grandpa deep down. They hadn't been very nice to Jen. Abby wouldn't want to go on holiday with them either if she were Jen.

Abby knew she wasn't much fun as a stepdaughter. She knew she was behaving like a brat. But she was fed up of trying to be polite and pretending these things didn't matter. They *did* matter. It was a relief, in a way, to stop pretending.

"Did you still want to watch *Legally Blonde*, Abby, love?" Jen said one evening. "We could watch it tonight if you wanted to?"

"No, thank you," Abby said stiffly.

"But, Abby," Dad said. "You told Jen you wanted to see it!"

"I've got homework," said Abby. It wasn't even a lie. She always had homework. She looked at Dad's shocked face and felt dreadful. "Maybe at the weekend," she said quickly. But she could see the disappointment in Jen's face, even though she quickly tried to hide it.

"Of course," Jen said. "The weekend would be lovely. Better even! We won't have to worry about being up too late. And I could get popcorn! I meant to get popcorn for today, and I forgot. But we don't have to watch it if you've changed your mind. That's OK too! Only if it's something you want. I know you're busy."

She went on and on and on.

Jen was pretending again. Abby knew it. She had seen the hurt in Jen's eyes. It made Abby boil. How could she believe anything this person said?

Did Jen even like her, or was she just pretending about that too?

Chapter 7
RUDENESS

Abby hated being rude. She hated being a brat. But now, somehow, she just seemed to turn into one around Jen. It was like Jen conjured up all the parts of Abby that she hated most.

"Do you have a birthday present for Halima?" Jen asked a few days after the conversation about the party. "I'm sorry – I don't know what your dad's rules are. Do we need to give you money to buy it, or do you do that yourself?"

"You don't give me *your* money," Abby said. "Dad gives me money – not you."

"Oh yes, of course," said Jen. "I didn't mean that – I just meant ..."

"Dad and I can fix it," said Abby. There wasn't anything to fix – she always bought presents out of her pocket money. And she didn't need a present anyway. But Jen didn't need to know that. Abby wondered if Jen would get offended, but she didn't. In fact, she was falling over herself to apologise again.

"I don't want to get in the way of you and your dad – you know that," Jen said. "I know I'm not your mum. I'm not trying to be. I just ..."

Abby longed for a real, proper fight – the kind she and Dad had sometimes. Why couldn't Jen say something real? Something she really felt? Something she *meant*? Why was it all just – just –

So fake?

*

The next time it happened was at the weekend. Dad was there.

"Abby, can you bring your dirty clothes down from your room, please?" Jen said. "I need to put a wash on."

"Sure," Abby said. She didn't look up from her phone.

"Abby?" Jen asked again.

"I said I'd do it!" Abby said. "Just let me read this."

Jen was quiet, but she didn't look happy. Abby finished reading the message and started writing a reply.

"Abby, can you do as Jen asked, please?" Dad said.

"I said I would!" Abby said.

"It's very kind of her to do your washing at all," Dad said. It was, Abby knew. Before Jen, Abby had done all her own laundry. Sometimes it didn't get done in time, and she had to wear dirty clothes to school.

"I never asked her to do my washing," Abby said. She could see Jen getting nervous.

"I don't mind you finishing your message," Jen said. "But I do need to put this wash on now before I go out. If I don't, you won't have a clean skirt for tomorrow ..."

"I can put it on," said Abby.

"Yes, but there are some of my clothes in there too which need to be done. I would be happier knowing it was on before I went out."

Abby stared at her phone. Why did she have to do it right now? Why did she have to do what Jen told her at all? What right did Jen have to come into her family and boss her around anyway?

The words *You're not my mum* hovered in Abby's mouth. It felt like a horrible cliché. She knew it was what all kids said to their stepmothers. But ... Jen *wasn't* her mum.

She'd always thought *You're not my mum* meant *You can't tell me what to do.* But in Jen's case, Abby meant *Stop pretending you love me. Be honest.*

But also, *You can't tell me what to do.*

"I will," she said. "Go out. I'll do it."

Jen looked anxious, and for once she stood her ground.

"I'd really rather it was done now," Jen said.

She looked properly worried. But why would someone care about clothes so much? What did it matter if Abby's skirt was dirty?

"Abby," said Dad. There was a warning tone in his voice. "Do as you're told."

"Of course, Dad," she said. She gave him a big smile. And she went to find her skirt.

Jen didn't say a word.

*

The next day, Jen didn't come home after school. She was going to the cinema with a friend, Dad said. Abby wondered if she would complain about her awful stepdaughter. The thought made her feel uncomfortable.

She'd never lived with someone who didn't love her before.

Dad made beans on toast and Angel Delight for tea. Afterwards, they did the washing-up together.

"Why are you being like this to Jen?" Dad said. "This isn't like my Abby."

Abby thought of all the reasons. They seemed too petty and complicated to try to explain to Dad. She shrugged.

"Don't you like Jen?" he said.

"I like her," said Abby. But it felt like the words meant less and less each time she said them. This felt like the saddest part of the whole thing. If Jen would just stop trying so hard, she could, really, honestly like her.

"I don't mean to be horrible," Abby said, rubbing a tea towel around a plate. "I just don't know how else to get her to back off."

"Maybe you should talk to her," Dad suggested.

Abby shook her head. "I can't!" she said. "Please don't make me." She hesitated. "Could you do it?"

"I already have," said Dad. "She is trying. She doesn't mean to get in your space. She's just nervous."

"But she's the grown-up!" said Abby. "What's she got to be nervous about?"

"Well, lots of things," said Dad. "She's moved into our house. We're a family, and she's an outsider ..."

"But that's just how *I* feel!" Abby said. She didn't mean the words to come out. Dad looked horrified.

"What do you mean?" he said.

Abby wished they'd never started this. "Nothing," she said. "Nothing, please, Dad. I didn't mean it. Talk about Jen instead."

"All right." Dad looked like he didn't believe her.

"As I said, she's insecure," he said. "She didn't have a fantastic dad like you do." He nudged Abby, who laughed, a little reluctantly. "She had a stepmother too when she was growing up – did she tell you that? But Jen's stepmother never really wanted her. I don't think her dad did either. Jen spent half her childhood trying to get her parents to like her. She wants to do it right for you."

"How can you not like your own kid?" said Abby, shocked.

Dad looked sad. "I don't know," he said. "But it's more common than you might think."

Abby thought about her friends. Did any of their parents not like them? Parents were supposed to like their kids. It was the rule, wasn't it?

Was Jen just nice because she wanted people to like her? Or was that really how she was? And if not, who was she really?

Abby felt guilty. And then she felt angry. Grown-ups weren't supposed to be complicated and messy! That was the kids' job! Grown-ups were supposed to have all this stuff figured out.

"What's the real Jen like?" Abby asked Dad.

Dad knew what she meant at once. "Well, I think she was being the real Jen when she told Gran and Grandpa it might be better for us to go on holiday without them. That was really hard for her."

"I suppose it's good that she could do that," said Abby. She sighed. She couldn't complain that Jen wasn't real and never had arguments and then complain when she *was* real and did stand up for herself.

"Gran's threatening to take you to Disneyland Paris just to get back at her," said Dad. "This could work out really well for you!"

Disneyland Paris! thought Abby. *Good old Gran.* She sat down at the kitchen table, trying to think.

"I do honestly, honestly think Jen's lovely," Abby said to Dad. "Really, I do. And I know she's kind, and I am grateful to her for washing my clothes and all that. I just hate it when she's so full on. I feel like I'm being squashed all the time. Do you feel like that?"

"Sometimes," Dad said. He was quiet for a moment, as if he was trying to work out how to explain it so Abby could understand. "Jen's trying so hard because she doesn't think you like her. Because you keep backing away, right?"

"I suppose."

"But you keep backing away because she's trying too hard."

"*Yes*," Abby said.

"So," said Dad, "I think there are two options. She could back off, then you won't feel so smothered. *Or.* You could be nicer to her, and maybe she won't feel so insecure."

Abby was silent.

"She should back off then," she said at last, a little sulkily. "She's the adult. I'm the child."

"I will tell her," said Dad. "But, Abby, listen, this is important. This is your house. You were here first. And you're always going to be the number-one person in my life. No matter what happens with Jen."

Abby felt her eyes fill with tears. She hadn't known that. Or ... maybe she had, but she hadn't let herself believe it.

"I know," she mumbled.

Abby took the saucepan from Dad and started drying it slowly. What would it be like to have parents who didn't like you? Abby couldn't imagine it. She and Dad argued and wound each other up sometimes. But Dad had always *liked* her. If your own *dad* didn't like you, it would feel like nothing was safe. It would be like living in a house made of paper.

Abby took the saucepan over to the kitchen cupboard and stowed it away. Thinking about how Jen grew up made Abby feel protective of her.

Chapter 8
A GIFT

The next day after school, Abby went home with Anna. Anna wanted to buy a birthday present for her mum, and Abby came along to keep her company. Their school was on the edge of the little town, and they had to walk along the high street to get home. Abby and her friends often stopped to buy sweets and crisps on the way back.

The town where they lived was often busy, especially in summer. It had lots of tearooms and gift shops, two hiking shops, and a shop that sold nothing but expensive chocolate. The high street was a good place to go if you wanted to buy someone a present.

Abby and Anna looked at the chocolate shop, but it was too expensive and not very interesting. They went round one of the gift shops and looked at all the rocks and crystals, but Anna said her mum didn't like crystals much.

"She doesn't like clutter at all," said Anna. "She's always trying to make me get rid of stuff."

"How about getting her something useful then," said Abby. "A mug?"

"I got her a mug last year," said Anna. She sighed. "My mum's just rubbish to buy for! She doesn't do anything, and she's always on a diet, so I can't even get her something to eat..."

"Smellies?" said Abby.

Anna groaned. "Boring. Mum is so boring."

Abby thought about Jen. She wasn't boring. She would like loads of the things in the gift shop. The tea towels with pictures of birds called Tit and Boobie on them would make her laugh. She would love the beautiful clay mugs and vases. She would be interested in the books on local history. Jen liked lots of things. She was interested in everything.

"Maybe I could buy Mum a tea towel," sighed Anna. "God, a tea towel! Who wants a tea towel for their birthday?"

At the front of the gift shop was a box with second-hand books in it. Abby looked through it. There was a boring-looking book about old churches, a copy of *Great Expectations* and …

It was a small, plain book with a red cover called *Gerry Goes to School* by Elinor M. Brent-Dyer. Abby picked it up. She recognised the author – it was the woman who wrote all the Chalet School books Jen liked so much. Was it another Chalet School book?

Abby turned it over. No, it wasn't. It was set in a completely different school – did Jen know this person had written other books? She supposed she must do – but Abby was sure she didn't have this one. She had two shelves of Chalet School books in the bookcase next to Dad's science-fiction books. She didn't have any other series.

Abby began to get excited. Jen wouldn't believe it if she got her this! She looked at the back of the book. It cost two pounds.

Her heart was racing. She took the book to the till. The woman behind the counter picked it up.

"Oh, school stories!" the woman said. "I used to love these when I was a girl. Malory Towers and St Clare's and all that!"

"Mm," Abby said, and tried not to look too interested.

"How much does this one cost?" the lady said, turning the book over. "Oh yes! Two pounds!"

Abby opened her purse and gave her the money. The lady smiled.

"Enjoy!" she said.

Abby's heart kept on racing. She turned to Anna, who was still looking glumly at tea towels.

"Coming?" she said. "Or are you buying those?"

Anna dropped the tea towel. "Even my mum *couldn't* want a tea towel," she said. "Let's go."

Outside the shop, Abby felt light and giddy with excitement. She loved buying people presents. But it was rare to find something so perfect.

"What are you so happy about?" said Anna.

"Nothing!" said Abby. She didn't want to explain about Jen. It would take too long. She gave Anna a big smile. "Come on," she said. "Let's buy your mum some bubble bath. Everyone likes bubble bath!"

*

Jen was in the kitchen when Abby came home. She was mopping the floor.

"Hi, darling!" Jen called. This time, Abby didn't even mind. She was too excited. She took the book out of her bag, put it behind her back and came into the kitchen.

"I've got something for you," Abby said.

"Oh?" Jen looked flustered. She was *worried*, Abby realised. She thought the something might be something bad. Abby felt suddenly ashamed.

"It's something good," she said.

Jen adjusted her face into a happy expression. But she still looked nervous. "Oh! Something good! OK!" she said.

"Look," Abby said, and held out the book so Jen could see it.

Jen's face changed. "Oh, Abby!" she cried.

"You don't have it, do you?" Abby asked.

"No, no!" Jen took the book and stared at it. "Wherever did you find it?"

"It was in a box of books in Cosy Corner. You know the little box they have with second-hand books in it? It was only two pounds! I had to pretend not to be excited. I didn't want the shopkeeper to realise it was valuable. It is valuable, isn't it?"

"It would certainly cost a lot more than two pounds on eBay!" Jen laughed. "These are even harder to find than the Chalet School books! Oh, Abby! Thank you!" She put her arm around Abby and hugged her. Abby didn't mind. Jen's happiness felt different this time. It felt real. Somehow, that made all the difference.

"Have you read it?" Abby asked. "The book, I mean?"

"No, never. I mean, I've read summaries, of course. I can't believe I get to read it for the first time! I feel about ten years old!"

They grinned at each other. Abby felt better about Jen than she had in ages.

Chapter 9
A DRESS

"What are you going to wear to Halima's party?" Jen asked Abby that evening.

"I don't know," Abby said. They were eating dinner. She stared at her jacket potato. She knew she should admit that there wasn't a party. But how could she say *I was lying to you*? Would Jen even want to know? Wouldn't it just be hurting her for no reason?

"You've got the school disco coming up too, haven't you?" said Jen. "What are you going to wear to that?"

"I don't know." Abby was grateful Jen had changed the subject. Abby had a clothing allowance, but she didn't get invited to loads of parties, so she didn't have many party clothes.

"I've got a dress I wore to last year's disco," Abby said. "But I think I've grown out of it."

"We should go shopping!" Jen said, looking excited. Really excited – not like she was pretending. "You and me. We could buy a dress – and some shoes ..."

"Really?" Abby said. She was surprised by how interested she was in this idea.

She loved Dad, but he was useless at shopping for clothes. He did his best, but he didn't really care. "You look lovely," he always said to every dress she tried on.

Mostly, Abby didn't miss having a mum at all. But she'd often wished for a mum to take her shopping. Other people's mums took them clothes shopping. She'd seen them when she was in town.

"Of course!" Jen said, and smiled at her. And this time when Abby smiled back, it felt real.

*

They went shopping on Saturday. Just the two of them.

"Where do you want to go?" Jen asked.

Abby shrugged. She'd thought Jen would do this part. "I dunno."

"Where do you normally get your clothes?"

"Online?" Abby said, feeling very small. This wasn't going to work. She needed Jen to suggest places, but Jen looked worried.

"Well, let's try the department stores," Jen said. "There's always lots of choice there."

Jen turned out to be right. The department store had a whole section full of party dresses.

"I can't wear these!" said Abby. "These are prom dresses. Not disco dresses."

"But they're lovely," Jen said. "Look at this one. Do you want to try it on?"

"Seriously?" Abby said. She looked at the dress. It was long and blue, with sequins and a big puffy lacy skirt. And it cost about three times as much money as she had.

"Why not?" Jen asked.

"Because I don't need a prom dress," Abby said. "And I can't afford it!"

Jen smiled. "Sometimes it's fun just to try things on," she said.

Perhaps it would be like a scene in a film, Abby thought. She'd try on the dress and suddenly she'd look beautiful. But she didn't. It was all wrong – too long and too stiff. She tried not to let her disappointment show.

"It doesn't quite work, does it?" said Jen. Abby was surprised. She'd thought Jen would say how nice it was. But no. Jen was being serious about this shopping trip. "Not to worry – let's see what else they have."

She went all over the shop, picking out dresses she thought Abby would like.

"How about this one?" Jen said. She showed Abby the dress. It was much shorter than the dresses Abby would normally wear. Weren't mothers supposed to want you to cover yourself up?

"It's not very ... me," Abby said.

"Try it and see," said Jen. "That's the fun of dress shopping. You get to try on all these different versions of yourself and see which one fits. Ooh, look! Jumpsuits! How about a black jumpsuit?"

"I don't know." Abby felt bewildered.

"Just try it!" said Jen.

It turned out Jen was right. Abby *did* feel different wearing the new clothes. More grown up. Prettier. Some of the outfits worked and some really didn't. But it was nice seeing all the different people she could be. In the end, Abby chose a simple green dress and a little black cardigan to go with it. It wasn't the sort of outfit she usually bought. But she felt like herself in it. A slightly more grown-up version of herself. Jen insisted on paying.

"My treat," Jen said. "Now shoes!"

Shoes were easier. They found some in the first shop they tried.

Afterwards, they went to a little cafe and ordered proper grown-up food – Jen had a salad and Abby had pasta. When she and Dad went out, they always got burgers or pizza. Kid food. Jen hadn't even suggested burgers. She was treating Abby like a grown-up, which Abby liked. Jen wasn't gushing either.

Afterwards, Abby had ice cream and Jen had a coffee.

"I feel as if things have gone wrong between us," Jen said.

Abby was shocked. She had never, ever expected Jen to come out and just say it.

Abby opened her mouth to say, "No, no, everything's fine." But then she shut it. That wasn't fair to Jen.

"A bit," Abby admitted.

"Your dad says you think I'm trying too hard," Jen said.

Abby felt herself getting hot. "No, no ..." she said.

"It's all right," said Jen. "You're not the only person who's said that to me. I just ... I want you to know how happy I am to be part of your family."

"But you've only just met me!" Abby said. "You can't possibly feel like that when we've just met!"

"It's been nearly half a year!" said Jen. "I do know you fairly well now."

"I suppose so." Abby looked down at her ice cream. "I just feel like I'm a toddler sometimes when you speak to me, as if you're telling me how lovely my picture is. The way you say that I'm so nice, or I'm doing so well at school ... it's like it doesn't mean anything. I hate it."

"Oh, Abby." Jen sounded upset. "I don't want you to feel like that! That's not what I mean at all! All those things – I do mean them. You know that, don't you? I just get nervous. I want things to be good between us so much. I want us to be a family. A happy family."

"I want that too," Abby said. It was the first time she'd realised that. It wasn't just *I like you* but also *I want you to keep living with us. I want us to be a family.* It surprised her, saying it out loud.

"Do you mean that?" Jen said. She sounded as surprised as Abby felt.

"Yes," said Abby. "I think I do."

"I will try," Jen said. "To give you some space, I mean. Perhaps you can tell me when I'm trying too hard?"

Tell Jen? Actually tell her when she was being annoying? Could Abby do that? Really?

"Or try to tell me, at least," Jen said. She smiled at Abby. "I know it's hard when you want someone to like you. I do like you, you know. Really."

"I like you too," said Abby. And for the first time, the words didn't feel like an apology. They felt real.

Chapter 10
THE AWARDS

The day of the awards ceremony came. Abby still hadn't said anything about the made-up party. She knew she should just tell the truth. But she couldn't.

Perhaps that made her a coward.

That morning, Jen bustled around the kitchen looking nervous, fussing about her dress and Dad's suit. Abby sat and ate her Rice Krispies and didn't say anything. Perhaps she could just pretend it didn't matter. Perhaps it didn't matter.

She put on her shoes and coat and found her schoolbag.

"I'm off now," she said.

"Bye, love!" said Dad.

Abby hesitated. Then she turned to go. "Good luck!" she said to Jen. And she shut the door behind her before Jen could answer.

She took her new outfit to school with her. She'd have to be wearing it when she came home or Dad and Jen might suspect that something was wrong. She'd already arranged to go to Halima's house after school.

She felt like a criminal.

Halima's house was as warm and friendly as ever. It was messier than Abby's, nosier too. Halima had a big brother who was always playing computer games in the living room. Halima's little brother never stopped talking.

"Did you know leeches have thirty-two brains?" Mohamed said, following them into the kitchen. "And octopuses have three hearts? And octopus tentacles have their own personality?"

"Shut up, Mohamed," said Halima. "Nobody cares."

"I care," said Abby. She liked Mohamed.

"So do I," said Halima's stepmum. She kissed Mohamed. "But maybe stop bothering Halima and her friend, OK?"

"Fiiine," said Mohamed. He took his book of animal facts and went into the living room to bother his big brother instead.

"Halima, did you finish your homework?" her stepmum said.

Halima sighed. "I've got Abby over!" she said.

"I'm sure Abby has homework too!" said Halima's stepmother. "You can do it together."

Halima pulled a face. "Is Jen like this?" she said to Abby.

"No," said Abby. Abby always did her homework. But Jen wouldn't have told her off if she didn't.

"Lucky you," said Halima.

Her stepmother said "Oi!" But she didn't seem cross.

"How is Jen anyway?" Halima's stepmum added. "Tell her I said hi. It's a thankless task, being a stepmother to teenagers."

"I am here, you know!" said Halima.

"Jen's fine," said Abby. "She's got this thing at work ... She won an award. She's pretty pleased."

"Tell her well done from me!" said Halima's stepmum. She sounded like she really meant it.

"OK," said Abby. The guilt about missing the award ceremony sat inside her like a stone.

"Come on," said Halima. "Let's go upstairs."

They went up to Halima's bedroom and sat on the bed together.

"My stepmum is *sooo* annoying," said Halima. She flopped down onto the bed and groaned. Abby sat next to her carefully. She had never spent much time just her and Halima. Normally, all their friends were there too. Perhaps Abby should have invited them too, but she hadn't felt like she could invite other people to someone else's house.

"Do you really hate her?" Abby asked.

Halima sighed. "No," she said. "Not really. It's just ... complicated. You know?"

"Oh yes," said Abby.

"And she isn't my mum. Life with her in it is different. Different in good ways and bad, you know?"

"*Yes*," said Abby.

Halima laughed. "I can like the good things and not the bad things," she said. "I can like her and miss how it was when it was just us. You can feel two things at the same time! Like, I love Mohamed, and he's also the most annoying child on the planet. I can feel both those things."

"I suppose so," said Abby. She hadn't thought of it like that before. But what Halima had said made a lot of sense. Jen was good. And Jen was difficult. Both those things could be true at the same time.

"My stepmum's all right really," said Halima. "Even if she is a pain in the bum."

Jen's awards ceremony started at 8 p.m. Her school was on the other side of town. It would take forty minutes to walk there. If Abby wanted to go, she'd have to leave at twenty past seven.

Could she go? If she did, would Jen and Dad guess that she'd been lying?

Perhaps it would be worse to go than not.

Perhaps it wouldn't.

That thought sat in Abby's head all evening. It sat there as she and Halima painted each other's nails and talked about school. It sat there as dinner smells wafted up the stairs.

"What time do you guys normally eat dinner?" Abby asked Halima.

Halima shrugged. "Whenever it's ready," she said.

Abby couldn't leave before dinner. Could she?

"Hang on a moment," Abby said, and went downstairs. Halima's stepmum was singing along to Radio 1 and stirring a pot.

"Hello, my lovely," she said as Abby came in. "Is everything all right?"

"Yeah." Abby hovered by the door. "What time is dinner going to be ready?"

"Not too long, sweetheart. Are you hungry?"

"No," Abby said. But Halima's stepmum seemed to know something was wrong.

"What's the matter?" she asked.

"Jen's award thing," Abby said. "It's today. At eight. At school. I wasn't going to go, but ... I think I'd like to."

"All right." Halima's stepmum didn't seem surprised. "Well, if you want, I can take you there in the car after dinner. We should get there about eight if the traffic isn't too bad. Does that work?"

"Yeah," Abby replied, smiling. How odd that she'd worried about this so much! Standing here in the kitchen, it all seemed easy.

*

Abby put on her new dress, the one she and Jen had chosen together. She put on her new shoes. She brushed her hair. Halima lent her some lip gloss and some purple eyeshadow. Abby didn't normally wear make-up, but she liked the way she looked wearing it. More grown-up somehow. More confident.

It was dark when Halima's stepmum pulled up to the school. But there were lights on in the main building and cars in the car park.

"Will you be OK from here?" she asked.

"I'll be fine, thanks," said Abby.

She felt awkward walking across the car park. What would Jen say when she saw her? She was bound to make a big fuss. She would probably never shut up about it.

Perhaps I should just go home, Abby thought. But she knew she wouldn't. She'd got this far.

It was ten past eight. The thing would have already started.

There was the school hall. There was the door. Abby took a deep breath. She opened the door and stepped inside.

A lady Abby didn't know was standing at the front of the hall talking. Everyone else was sitting in seats. Dad was at the back. Abby went and sat beside him. He didn't say anything, but he gave her a small smile.

"The winner of best Maths teacher ..." the woman at the front was saying.

Abby smiled at Dad and settled back in her seat to watch.

Chapter 11
AND AFTER

After it was all over, Jen came up to Abby and Dad.

"Abby! How lovely that you're here!" she said. But Jen seemed a bit distracted. She hugged Abby. Then she hugged Dad.

"Well done," he said. "Do you want to get out of here?"

"We can't!" said Jen. She looked worried, Abby thought. "Can we? Wouldn't it be rude?"

"Of course we can," said Dad. He put his arm around Jen. "Let's go and get ice cream," he said.

They went to the ice-cream parlour on the high street and got chocolate sundaes.

Abby had thought Jen would gush and gush about her coming. But she didn't. She just wanted to talk about the awards.

"Are you sure it was all right to rush off like this? They won't think it was rude?"

"They won't even notice," said Dad.

"Oh, that was horrible!" Jen cried. "I felt so embarrassed up on that stage, with everyone looking at me. Did I sound awful when I did my speech?"

"Not at all." Dad looked proud. "You were great."

"You were," said Abby. Jen had been fine. She'd done a short speech about being a librarian, and how much she loved her job. Abby couldn't see what she was bothered about. But she looked so worried about it, even now. Abby felt strangely protective. For the first time, she didn't feel like she needed to pull away from Jen. If anything, she wanted to pull Jen closer to her.

"I'm so glad it's over!" said Jen.

*

Nobody had exactly said that Jen was going to be here for ever, but Abby could see that things were serious. Dad and Jen weren't engaged or anything like that. They had booked a summer holiday, in the Lake District of all places. (Disneyland Paris was definitely going to be better.) And they'd accepted an invitation for a wedding that was nearly a year away. Jen was looking more and more like she was going to be a permanent feature.

Abby wondered if she and Jen would ever be friends. Would Abby ever think of her as her mother? It was an odd thought. But not as odd as it would have been a couple of months ago. Abby could sort of see how it might work.

Things were better between Abby and Dad too. A couple of weeks after the awards ceremony, Dad knocked on the door of Abby's room.

"Can I talk to you about something?" he said.

"Sure." It sounded serious. Abby shut her laptop.

"I've decided to give up going to choir," Dad said. "It was fun for a while, but it's not really my sort of thing."

"OK," said Abby. She wondered where this was going.

"Jen's still going to go," Dad said. "So, I thought ... well ... we could have Wednesdays as *our* night. Just you and me. If you wanted to."

Dad looked at Abby hopefully. She realised he thought she might *not* want to!

"I'd love that," Abby said. He looked relieved.

"We could watch *Ms. Marvel*," she said.

"And *Deep Space Nine*," said Dad.

"And we could go to the cinema," Abby added. "Just you and me, like we used to."

"And get pizza!" said Dad. Jen didn't like pizza. She thought it was unhealthy.

"I've missed you," Abby said suddenly. She hadn't meant to say it out loud. It just came out. Dad's eyes went soft.

"I've missed you too," he said. "I thought ... maybe you were getting too old to want to spend time with me."

"And I thought you were more interested in Jen!" said Abby. They grinned at each other a bit shyly.

"Do you really mind her living here so much?" said Dad.

"I liked it better just us," Abby admitted.

"That's fair," said Dad.

"But I do like Jen," said Abby. "I'd miss her if she went. I liked going shopping with her. I'm glad I went to her awards ceremony."

Dad raised his eyebrow at her. Abby wondered if he was going to ask if there had really been a party. But he didn't.

"We can make this work, can't we?" Dad said instead.

"Can we stop trying so hard to make it work?" said Abby. "It's fine. I like you. I like her. We have pizza. Isn't that enough?"

"More than enough," said Dad. He kissed her. "I'm so lucky to have you both," he said.

"Me too," said Abby. And right at that moment, she meant it.

Our books are tested
for children and young people by
children and young people.

Thanks to everyone who consulted on
a manuscript for their time and effort in
helping us to make our books better
for our readers.